I0624334

Hostile Environments
More Stories for the Worst in All of Us

By Fran Maglione

Copyright © 2017 Fran Maglione

All rights reserved.

ISBN-13: 978-0996864619

Cover design by Kevin Monahan

For all the kids in school no one liked,
who grew up to be the adults no one likes.

CONTENTS

GLORIA'S HOME

Gloria stirred awake to the sound of something sharp ripping and pulling on the sheets next to her on the bed. It sounded like the cat had returned and was tearing at the sheets with his claws, trailing all the way up to her head. She kept her eyes closed willing herself to go back to sleep or for the cat to go away. Of course, Gloria knew that the second she did open her eyes the cat would be gone - just a shadow in her peripheral vision.

Though, lately, everything was starting to feel like that.

Finally, she opened her eyes and saw the shadow figure dart behind her pillow. She didn't bother reaching over and looking for it; she knew it was gone. Perhaps the cat just wanted some company in the early morning hours. It had probably been alone in this house for years before Gloria arrived.

The house was large as well, making it easy for creatures to hide in its corners. It was an old New England colonial with creaky wooden floors and drafty windows. It needed a lot of work, but it was a real find for the price and the neighborhood. Gloria sat up in her bed and tried to stretch, but the constant kink in her neck and shoulders prevented her from lifting her arms. It was a miserable feeling, but Gloria was almost used to it at this point.

She was never hungry when she woke up, but there was always food waiting for her on the table. Philip always made sure she never went hungry throughout the day. She rarely saw him anymore. They were like two ships passing in the night, but he made his presence known in the house whenever he could. Gloria tried not to think about how much longer they would be able to keep this charade going. It worked for now, and that was all she needed.

Gloria floated down the stairs on light feet, consciously avoiding the creaky parts of the steps. The noises made her head hurt. When she reached the first floor, she ducked her head in preparation for the red-tailed hawk that often circled the ceiling on this floor. As expected, it dove right by her, releasing its shrill cry.

Gloria stood in silence, watching the majestic bird soar around her, never even having to flap its wings. It was no wonder the cat always stayed on the second floor. The cat and the hawk would probably not get along very well, she thought. Once she reached the kitchen she padded over to the table, peering at the cold plate of food left behind for her. She picked up a piece of toast, nibbled it lightly, then made some tea. She was soon distracted by a loud thumping sound coming from outside.

Gloria ran to the dining room window and saw a large black bear bounding down the hill next to her house. Once it reached the street an even bigger brown bear appeared from across the way and tackled the black bear. The two bears roared and clawed each other while Gloria stood and watched, continuing to eat her toast.

As if pulled outside by a force, a young woman walked out of the house across the street and approached the bears. The woman pulled out a camera and started snapping photos of the two bears fighting until the flash alerted them to her presence. The brown bear took one look at the woman and pounced, the black bear temporarily forgotten. Gloria just stared as the bear clamped its jaws around the woman's neck and took off running down the street, dragging the woman along. The black bear watched them disappear down the street before turning and stomping in the opposite direction.

Without a word, Gloria turned away from the window and walked back to the kitchen. She poured herself a cup of tea and sat down at the table, focusing on the color of the steeping tea and the steam lightly rising from it and into her face. She sighed loudly, forcing herself not to move or look around at the shadows now whirling around her.

One such shadow was of a small animal prowling around the perimeter of the room. It kept circling her menacingly as other shadows began joining it. Pretty soon there was a carousel of animal shadow figures circling Gloria in the kitchen.

She sat at the table with her head down, eyes welling with tears and her lips trembling.

"Go away," she pleaded. "Go away, go away, go away!"

She slammed her fist down on the table, causing a splash of tea from her mug to spill. Above her, the hawk circled once more and screeched. It seemed to focus its attention on one of the animal shadows then swooped down and scooped up the shadow before flying into another room.

"Good," Gloria muttered, "you're finally being useful."

The house had long ago taken on a life of its own. Gloria had made peace with that, or so she thought. It never got easier to live in a home that had all the control and felt different every day. The shadows emerged the same way every day, and the cat and hawk stayed the same, but the house always felt new. It felt tense, confused, juvenile, and angry. Gloria couldn't make heads or tails of it most of the time. She heard new voices, saw new faces, and always felt constricted and imprisoned. She was trapped.

It had never truly frightened her before now, though. It always simply seemed irritating or odd, but lately it was downright scary. And as if summoned by her thoughts, the light pouring in through the windows dimmed, a dull thud sounded in the background, and a cold breeze wafted inside. Everything was imploding around her, and Gloria could barely hold on.

The thudding grew louder until it reached the back door and Gloria panicked. She didn't know what foul creature was coming for her now, but she decided that she didn't want any part in it. She jumped from her seat and bolted to the entryway of the house, pulling open the hall closet door and squeezing herself inside. She quietly pulled the door shut and crouched down among the coats and rain boots just as the back door burst open.

Pulling her knees up to her chin and wrapping her arms around herself she rocked back and forth as she heard large feet stomping inside, making the entire house shake. Where was Philip? Gloria asked herself. He would know what to do. He always seemed to know what she needed. He took care of her.

Gloria peered out of the crack in the door to watch what was happening. She saw a giant beast with hooves for feet, a powerful upper body and horns on his head. His skin was tinted red and he stood monstrously tall. Gloria predicted around 10 feet or so, as he had to duck to avoid hitting his head on the ceiling. He was holding a bowl of human limbs. With a quick glance around the room, the beast decided to sit down at the table. He picked up an arm from the bowl and started eating, gnawing the meat off of the bone and chomping it hard with his fangs. He slurped and chewed loudly as he feasted on his breakfast.

Gloria remained in the hall closet, wide-eyed and watching. She held her hand over her mouth to stop from vomiting. She tried to keep her whimpers and heavy breathing as quiet as possible as the creature ripped and sucked at the fatty meat on the bones. Finally, the beast rose from the table and stomped back outside, licking his fingers along the way. With a sigh, Gloria stood up and exited the closet, her legs and knees feeling cramped and sore.

She stumbled back to the kitchen shaking with tears in her eyes. The stale odor of rotting flesh was still heavy in the kitchen making her dry heave. She ran to the den to escape the rank smell, just barely dodging the hawk that soared over her. Gloria collapsed on the couch and sobbed, deciding then and there that she had enough.

The house needed to be stopped, she thought.

Gloria took a deep breath and stood, confidently making her way to the stairs. When she reached the top, she turned into her bedroom and over to her vanity desk, which was covered in candles. She grabbed her book of matches and lit one. Then without hesitation, she held the lighted match underneath one of the drapes at the window until it caught fire.

The flames rose quickly and spread all around her, catching on every bit of fabric and furniture in the room. It spread across the walls and caught onto the bed linens before traveling across the carpet and out the bedroom door. Within moments, the entire house was engulfed in flames. Heavy smoke filled the room, but it didn't seem to bother Gloria.

She sat at her vanity desk and picked up her hair brush. She looked at herself in the mirror and admired her bright blonde hair. After gathering it up with her hands and laying it over her shoulder, she began brushing it slowly.

As the brush glided softly over Gloria's hair, she began humming her favorite song. The music reverberated through the burning house as she continued staring at herself in the mirror and smiling. Around her, the house burned.

She briefly wondered what would become of all the animals.

*****

Philip stood in front of the cold steel door, peering in through the small barred window and watching a stocky, balding middle-aged man in a straightjacket sitting on the floor humming to himself. There was never a dull moment with this particular patient, and in Philip's 10-year career as a nurse practitioner at this asylum, he had never met another patient quite like this one.

His fellow nurse on duty, Michael, walked toward Philip and

stood next to him in front of the door.

"So, who is he today?"

"Gloria's home today," Philip said with a fond smile. He let out a quiet chuckle and shook his head. He always liked the Gloria character.

"Well, the patient in 203 seems agitated. We're worried that he's going to get a little violent so we'll need another set of hands," Michael said.

"Okay, sure, let's go," Philip answered quickly, snapping out of his trance from watching the patient.

The two nurses hurried down the hallway, not looking back. The bald man in the room continued humming a cheerful tune and swaying back and forth on the floor as he stared at the wall in front of him with a look of pure ecstasy.

WAKE UP GRANDMA

"Can we wake up grandma yet?"

We really can't spoil our little princess enough, in my opinion. I can't say no to her sweet smile, piercing blue eyes, soft golden curls - she was all delicate limbs and melodic giggles, twirling and dancing around the room. She turned seven years old today and we just couldn't resist overwhelming her with presents and love.

The dead raccoon was an instant favorite. She held it in her arms and stroked its filthy, matted-down fur. She named it Fred.

And although she had really wanted that pig fetus in a jar, we just couldn't find any. Every store was sold out, but I'm not surprised. It was a popular item this year. But the real standout was the box full of human organs. I scolded my father for splurging on such a frivolous item.

"That must have cost you a fortune," I sighed. "You really do spoil her."

My father chuckled and shook his head.

"I'm supposed to! I'm her grandfather."

My wife took out her camera.

"Okay, Penny, give me a big smile!"

Penny held up her raccoon carcass with pride, a cheesy grin

plastered on her face as the shutter clicked.

"Can we wake up grandma now?" she asked.

"Not yet, pumpkin, it's still early," I answered. "Grandma needs her rest. You know that."

With a huff, Penny dropped the corpse on the rug, grabbed the box of organs and ran out of the room. My father laughed over his bowl of maggots as he spooned more into his mouth.

"That girl is such a ball of energy," he mumbled.

I never knew where she got it from. I'd been a shy, quiet child and my wife was always very reserved. I guess when the world gives you a beautiful daughter, you just want to do everything you can to make her believe she can conquer the world.

I stood up and sliced a few more pieces off the roast. One by one they slithered down and splashed into the pool of blood that had settled on the bottom of the serving platter. I stabbed a piece with a fork and swirled it around in the blood before slapping it onto my plate. That's where all the vitamins came from, my mother would always tell me.

Suddenly, I heard our dog whimpering on the floor next to me.

"Honey, did you feed Rascal?"

"Oops! I'm sorry, Rascal!" my wife jumped up from her chair and jogged over to the dog. "With all of the party excitement it slipped my mind. Come on, sweetie."

She led the dog by the collar to the front door. As she opened it, Rascal bolted outside like he was on fire, mouth foaming and salivating.

"Mommy, take my picture!"

We turned and saw Penny stroll back into the room with intestines wrapped around her hips like a belt, and an oozing liver dripping blood and other fluids placed atop her head. The crimson blood mixed with her golden curls and trickled onto her dress. A beautiful picture, indeed. My father and I laughed while my wife snatched her camera back up and clicked the shutter over and over, beaming with pride.

"My little princess!" she laughed.

Moments later the dog returned to the front door, covered in blood and with an arm dangling in his mouth. He was calmer and satiated. I laughed and shook my head.

"Looks like we'll be getting a new mailman again!"

"He really seems to like how they taste," my wife nodded. "Should we wake up your mother now?"

"Yes! Let's wake up grandma!" Penny squealed.

I glanced at my watch.

"Not yet," I said. "Grandma needs more rest. We'll wake her in a bit, I promise."

A car pulled into the driveway and my wife stood and squinted out the window.

"Oh, good, my parents are finally here. They must've hit so much traffic. They were supposed to be here an hour ago!"

"I'm not surprised, what with the festival and all," I said.

Our daughter's birthday coincided with the town's annual summer festival. Traffic becomes pretty congested throughout the day, but the streets are practically impassible once they release the elephants.

It's such a beautiful festival, though, and with the magic of the season and the scent of fresh blood in the air, it's basically impossible not give into the urge to procreate. Now Penny gets to share her birthday with it, at least.

My wife opened the front door as her parents waddled through with their arms loaded with large presents, blurting out apologies for their tardiness.

"Oh, stop, it's okay!" my wife grabbed a gift from her mother's hands. "Let me help you. My goodness, did you buy out an entire toy store?"

"Grandma! Grandpa!" Penny came bounding into the foyer, the entrails around her waist leaking onto the tiled floor. "Yay, more presents!"

My in-laws placed their gifts on the table and each gave my daughter a hug and a kiss before making their way around the room to greet the rest of us.

I glanced at my watch.

"I suppose we should wake my mother now."

My father nodded at me and stood up, making his way to a hall closet. My wife followed close behind, grabbing some candles from the top shelf and the bowl of salt. I set to work drawing the pentagram with a piece of chalk on the floor.

Penny skipped in circles around us as my wife lit the candles and my father started his chanting. My in-laws reclined in their seats, watching us and enjoying their cocktails. The thick red liquid dribbled down their chins as they talked quietly among themselves.

"I wonder what grandma got me for my birthday," Penny said as the house began to quake.

My father chanted louder as the candle flames burned stronger. I sat next to my father and chanted with him as my wife tore off her clothes and wailed, flailing her arms about and knocking over the candles, watching their flames ignite the rest of the house.

The smoke thickened as it billowed around the room. My father-in-law began coughing loudly and politely excused himself. It had been a while since his last incantation so I'm sure he wasn't used to it anymore. There's never any need for apologies in our house, though. We love each other through all of our faults.

As the fire blazed around us while my daughter giggled with glee, I smiled wide - my heart full of love and contentment. I've always loved making family memories, and we'd remember this birthday for a long time.

"Happy birthday, princess," I whispered as the floor opened beneath us and two giant claws appeared, tearing through the floorboards.

Penny squealed with delight.

"Grandma's awake!"

HAPPY FAMILY

I hate that bitch in the dark green van.

I've always hated her since the day I first saw that stupid van pull sharply in front of me after barely even pausing at a stop sign. She didn't even look; she just pulled out into the road as if the entire planet was expected to move out of her way and welcome her with loving, open arms.

Thankfully, she didn't have a vanity plate. I think if she had a vanity plate I would have had to run her off the road. But, it was a normal license plate. No bumper stickers either, mind you. There was only one thing about the car itself that threw me into a rage: she had those stick figure family stickers affixed to the rear window of the van.

Who does that? I mean, really. Nobody cares how many kids you have, or how many pets you have, or what your husband's hobby is. He likes to golf. Great, want a trophy? Oh, and your 4-year-old daughter is a little ballet dancer? How unique and out of the ordinary! I'm sure one day she'll be President of the United States.

I started seeing that stupid van every single morning. I don't mean on occasion, randomly, or every so often. I mean every single goddam day of the week when I drove into work I somehow got stuck behind that dark green hulking ship of a car covered in ridiculous stick figures.

Wow, you have a dog? Really? And your son plays baseball? What a lucrative and vivacious life you all must share! You're clearly the family of the century. Too bad you drive like an inebriated monkey who was just punched in the face after riding a merry-go-round for 45 minutes.

Today feels different, though. Something is off, and it's not good. I have a bad feeling that flows through my very bones. I caught up to your van as usual that Monday morning, and stared at the lifeless stick figures on your rear window as I drove to work. There's a father, a mother, two sons, a daughter, and a dog. What a happy little family.

*****

Several days have gone by and I haven't seen your van. I'm starting to worry a little bit now. Maybe that feeling in my gut wasn't just a feeling after all. But how could anything be wrong? I don't even know you. You're just a dark green van in front of me as I trek to my job every morning. Surely nothing has happened.

A week goes by and I don't see your van. I become legitimately concerned until, finally, the day arrives. At 16 days later, I see your van return to the road in front of me. I pull up behind you feeling comforted by your presence until I make a sharp realization.

One of the boy stick figure stickers has been removed from your window.

I gasp in shock initially before quickly regaining my senses. It's just a sticker, I think to myself. You probably went through a car wash and it came off. Those stickers are cheap and poorly made. They're not meant to last forever.

The next few days go as planned. I drive to work and see your dark green van driving ahead of me. We're both going to the same general area. We both have jobs to do in order to pay for these cars we're driving. Everything is as it should be.

Finally, Thursday morning arrives and I drive into work as usual, but your green van is suspiciously absent. Oh, God, I think, not again.

Two weeks later, your car returns absent another sticker. This time, it's the little girl sticker. The ballerina, right? She was your little dancer, and now she's gone. Just like that. What on earth is happening in that family? For a brief moment I wonder if I should call the police, but then I look at the window more closely. The outline of the sticker is still clearly there. There is even still part of an arm. They must just be going to a bad car wash or something. That's clearly all it is. There isn't some family slowly killing off their own children, right? That couldn't possibly be it.

Suddenly you're gone for an entire month. I'm thrown into a panic. I realize that something is definitely not right. This is not a normal occurrence - this is something that must be noted. Something is, indeed, going on at the home of the dark green van driver.

But then one day you're back again - dark green van shining brightly in the sun, with only two stickers left: a husband and wife. The three children and the dog are gone. When did the dog leave? How did I miss that one? Were they reluctant parents? Did these people systematically kill off their entire family? Are they happier alone?

When I get to work that morning I pick up the phone and am about to dial 9-1-1 when my boss calls me into a meeting. I sigh and hang up the phone then reluctantly make my way into the conference room. I will solve this mystery another day. It's just stickers, I keep telling myself. I'm taking this too far.

*****

Nearly an entire season has gone by and I haven't seen your van. It's autumn now and the leaves have changed, yet I haven't seen you. Are you okay? Are you alive? I have no idea what's going on, or if it's even anything I need to be worried about.

Finally, the day has come again. It's the end of October now and a crisp, cold wind has started blowing in and rustling the leaves off their branches. But none of that matters because you're here now. I've been worried and missing you, not knowing exactly what you've been going through. I wish I could talk to you, dark green van lady, and find out what has been happening in your life.

There's only one sticker left on the back of your car, and it's you. It's a sticker of a mother, wearing an apron, holding a plate of cupcakes. Do you like to bake cupcakes? Did you bake them for your family? Where is your family, green van driver? I want to know. I want to learn all about you.

*****

Today is the day, my darling van driver. I will find out who you are and talk to you. I feel a connection to you - one that I've never felt before. I want to make sure you're okay, and that you're taken care of. A lot has happened in the last few months, and I'm very worried about you. Maybe you could vent to me and share with me all that you've been going through. I might even be able to help.

But before I even get the chance to talk to you, I drive my normal route to work and see you on the side of the road. The dark green van is toppled over, having rolled several times off the street and into the embankment. It looks like you've hit a tree. Cars slow down as they roll past you, but nobody stops to see if you need help. They all assume you're just fine, or that someone else will help. I know better, though.

Before the police can arrive, I pull over to the side of the road. I get out of my car and slowly approach the van. I can see you in the passenger's seat. You have your seatbelt on, so that's good, but there's blood oozing from your head and your ears, and you're not moving. I know you're dead without even having to touch you. I shed a tear knowing that I will never get to talk to you, to understand you, to learn to love you instead of hate you.

I walk to the back of your upside-down van and approach the window. I reach over to the one stick figure sticker that's left on the rear window. I grab the head of the mother stick figure and slowly peel her off the window.

With the sticker still affixed to my finger, I walk back to my trunk. I pop it open and reach inside for my trusty notebook. I open it and add your sticker to the collection of all the other stickers from the back of your van: the two boys, the girl, the dog, the father. They're all there, you know, so I add you to the rest of them so that you can be a family again. A perfect little stick figure family, right?

I toss the notebook back into my trunk. It bumps against that axe I have, still covered in dried blood. I really should clean that off. And look, there's those pruning shears I have, and that piece of brake line I cut from your van. It's all there, you see, tucked together and comfortable like a close-knit happy family.

I hope you're truly happy now. I know I am.

FRAN MAGLIONE

BACHELOR PARTY

Pounding bass reverberated through the city streets. The clacking of expensive dress shoes echoed along the sidewalk as the four men approached the club, straightening their ties and picking lint off their suit coats. The bachelor party for their friend was underway.

They laughed and slapped each other's backs as they walked up to the entrance, loudly announcing their presence to the bouncer out front. Their hands smacked the shoulders and back of the bachelor telling the bouncer how important he was tonight and that they were going to show him a good time. Their yells and cheers made the bouncer chuckle. The $100 bill one of the men slipped into his hand sealed the deal, and the velvet ropes parted.

A day full of 36 layoffs, massive pay cuts (not for them), and several disgruntles having to be escorted out by security probably would have left other men shaken. But all that mattered that night was their friend having breasts in his face and an ass in his lap to prepare him for the rigors of married life. They would be the first to tell you that it's a brutal existence - just ask any of their mistresses.

The men were immediately led into a back room by a short blonde with a big smile. The music was blaring, and thanks to some pre-gaming the men were already drunk before they even ordered their first round of shots. But, again, none of that mattered - it was their associate's bachelor party and no expense was to be spared.

Four women sat silently in the dressing room putting the finishing touches on their mascara and red lipstick. One of them adjusted her cleavage in her sequin top, and another added more glitter to her eyelids. They took one last look at each other and smiled before heading out to the private room. They knew they were going to do well that night.

Waitresses moved about the room in a flurry, refilling glasses and avoiding grabby advances. The men had only just arrived but had already taken over practically the entire establishment. They handed out wads of cash like they were passing around pieces of gum, so everyone was eager to please them. Within minutes, the owner of the club came over to personally greet them and give them each a fat cigar. He snapped his fingers at a couple of the waitresses sending them running to the back room to get the real top-shelf bottles.

Suddenly, the lights dimmed. The owner laughed and clapped his hands. He summoned the remaining servers and led them out of the room as he smiled and ensured the men they were about to have the time of their lives.

The men were already obliterated, slumping over in their chairs and hitting each other and laughing. The bachelor was ecstatic, cheering loudly and demanding for the show to begin. Slowly, a spotlight illuminated on the small stage in front of them.

The first woman stepped out, hair wild and curly and a tattoo of a fox sitting prominently on her arm. The music started up, and the woman began rolling her hips in time with the music. The men erupted into cheers.

She smiled at the reaction and slowly began pulling off her top. The men unleashed every inappropriate word they had ever learned from drunk uncles or porn videos. As the whistling and hooting continued, a second woman sidled on stage. They were soon joined by the two other women.

The loudest of the men laughed and called to the bachelor, pointing out that one of the women bore a striking resemblance to the office assistant he slept with at a conference two months ago. The men all erupted into laughter as the bachelor blushed and shook his head.

Alcohol splashed onto the stage as the men cheered and gestured drunkenly with their drinks. Dollar bills trickled down around the women like snowflakes. The four of them exchanged smiles, and then slowly pranced down from the stage and toward the men.

The woman with the fox tattoo approached the bachelor like a predator hunting its dinner. He could barely get a word out as the woman slowly straddled his lap and started to wiggle her hips. The other men cheered and encouraged the woman, telling her to give him the best final night of freedom she possibly could. One of the men threw a wad of cash at her, hitting her on the side of the head. The men laughed. She exchanged another glance with the three other women as they straddled the laps of the remaining members of the party.

The music was blaring and no one could hear what was being said, if there was anything worth hearing anyway. Strobe lights flashed and blinded them. The men could barely form coherent sentences, but it didn't stop them all from demanding more shots. No waitresses came back into the room, though. They were alone with the women as far as they could tell.

The men continued making more drunken demands, and their words became angrier and more aggressive as time went on. More clothes should be removed. The music was too loud. Their drinks were empty. One even asked how much it would cost to bring them all back to a hotel room for a night. The lead woman silently removed her skirt instead.

Following her lead, the other women silently stripped down and resumed their positions on the men's laps. That made them all shut up.

With a final crooked smile, the lead woman sat up in the bachelor's lap and glanced around at the other women. They all smiled at her as her eyes turned red and her fangs appeared, glistening in the dim club lights. She leaned down and buried her fangs into the bachelor's neck.

His shout was drowned out mostly by the pulsating music, and the other women continued their gyrating ministrations in the laps of the men, distracting them from the feeding. One by one all of their eyes returned to their natural red, and they hissed as their fangs grew in their mouths.

The men were confused and frightened as they tried to figure out what was now sitting in their laps. The beautiful dancing women were now faceless demons with sharp talons and charred, scaly skin. Their blood red eyes seemed to glow in the dark room.

The men only had a brief moment to scream before the demons tore their bodies to shreds. Muscle and skin hung from the demons' mouths as they feasted. The deafening music preventing any noises from reaching anyone in the front of the club. The owner and the waitresses still stayed away from the room, letting the men get their full money's worth.

Once they were satiated and nothing remained of the men but bones and fabric scraps, the leader stood on its hind claws and licked the blood off its face with its forked tongue. Together the four of them transformed back into female forms, looking slightly different this time in hair color and facial features, but still in the form of women. The leader kept the fox tattoo every time it transformed, though.

They picked up their scattered clothing and headed back to the dressing room to grab the rest of their belongings. Together they walked out into the night air, strolling peacefully down the sidewalk and discussing how they would get their next hearty meal.

IN STEREO

The crunch of dried leaves beneath the soles of Anna's running sneakers echoed through the park as she jogged along the path. Strands of brown hair that escaped her ponytail clung to her sweat-covered forehead as she glided along, stepping in time with the music blaring through her earbuds. As the song came to an end Anna slowed to a walk, stopping fully once she reached a park bench.

She smiled and said hello to one of her neighbors from the apartment building sitting across the way. She waved to Phil, the man who always walked his dog at the same time each day. And she happily greeted Mrs. Dunston, an old woman who lived a few blocks away from her, when she saw the woman slowly walk by on her daily afternoon stroll.

"Winter will be here before we know it," Mrs. Dunston said with a smile, as she pulled her shawl tighter around herself. "I can feel the chill in the air!"

"I'm certainly not rushing it," Anna said with a chuckle as Mrs. Dunston continued on her way.

Anna bent over the park bench in an attempt to stretch out her cramped side, but a glint of something shiny under the bench caught her attention. On closer inspection she saw that it was a brand new pair of stereo headphones, shiny and black with chrome details. They were even wireless. She reached down and grabbed them.

"Oh, wow, these are awesome!" she said out loud as she tore off her own sub-par earbuds and crammed them into the pocket of her sweatshirt.

She looked at the headphones in her hands, turning them over and checking for damage. They looked to be in perfect condition. With an excited smile, Anna placed them on her head to see how they fit.

The shrill blast of a woman's scream exploded through the headphones and pounded Anna's eardrums. She flung the headphones off her head and stood there in shock, wondering what caused that screaming sound.

She picked the headphones back up and looked them over. Then she looked at her MP3 player. Maybe it was simply a bad connection and she needed to sync them correctly. Maybe it was just feedback, like an electric guitar squealing through an amplifier. There had to be something wrong with it. Headphones don't just scream.

As Anna began poking around the headphones, she suddenly stopped and wiped her hands on her shorts.

"I don't know where these have been," she said with a grimace. She turned on her heels and headed back home to give them a quick cleaning before attempting to program them correctly.

Back at her apartment, Anna programmed them to her home stereo to see if they worked better that way. She put the headphones on and was once again startled by a sharp, piercing scream.

Straining from the noise, she quickly tossed the headphones to the floor. A dull ring permeated through her head for a few moments.

"No wonder somebody left these behind. They're clearly busted."

Anna tossed them into her trash bin next to her desk and headed for the shower.

*****

Anna turned on the television and headed to her small kitchen to start making dinner. As she filled a pot with water, she listened to the local news broadcasting in the background.

"Police still have no leads in the mysterious murder of a young woman last night," the news anchor said, "but they have released the 911 recording of the victim's last words. Police traced the call for help to a payphone at Rogers Park."

Anna froze. She had just been in Rogers Park for her run. She remembered where those old payphones were, too, as she always ran right past them. A chill ran up her spine and she shuddered. Just as she resumed preparing dinner, she heard the 911 call recording playing on the news. She heard a frantic woman's voice saying someone was following her and she was scared. Then suddenly the woman screamed and the line went dead.

Dropping the box of pasta she was holding, Anna ran back into the living room.

"That scream," she said. "It's the scream! It has to be."

Anna immediately dug into the trash bin and pulled out the headphones. She put them on her head but heard nothing. Anna sighed heavily.

"What is wrong with me today?"

She put the headphones down on her desk and walked back into the kitchen to finish making her dinner.

When she was finished, she plopped down on the couch with the headphones, trying to find somewhere to pry them open. Maybe they just needed a quick repair, she thought. Perhaps something was loose or bent. On a whim, she put them on again, and was shocked by a male voice now screaming through the headphones. She pulled them off and stared at them in disbelief.

"I don't understand. What is this supposed to mean?"

Feeling exhaustion and confusion overtake her, she put the headphones down and headed to bed. There was nothing she could do about it tonight.

*****

The next morning, Anna woke up feeling groggy and anxious. After tossing and turning all night, she went to brew some coffee and flipped on the morning news.

"Police are baffled once again by yet another murder in Rogers Park," the anchor reported.

Anna's stomach dropped.

"Witnesses reported seeing a young man jogging through the park yesterday evening, and then disappearing after turning a corner near some bushes. The witnesses claimed to hear him scream loudly."

"Oh, God," Anna breathed.

She stared wide-eyed at the headphones still sitting on the couch.

"People are dying and I can hear them," she said. "Why is this happening?"

Anna started trembling.

"Is it for me?" she asked no one. "Are the screams a warning and I'm supposed to do something about them?"

Realization quickly dawned on her.

"Yes. I'm supposed to help these people," she said, determination battling her fear. "I found these headphones for a reason. I have to find the killer."

Forgetting the coffee, Anna threw on some jeans and a hoodie, grabbed the headphones, and ran out the door heading back toward the park.

When she arrived, she headed immediately to the area where she originally found the headphones. She looked around for anything suspicious. As she walked along her normal jogging route she saw a dark figure walking through the trees. It was a large man wearing baggy, black clothing. He had a thick, dark beard and scraggly hair. He was definitely the most suspicious looking person at the park, so Anna followed him.

He walked along the sidewalk out of the park and down the street. Anna continued following him at a distance for several blocks. The man never looked behind him, but anytime he shifted or looked to the side she would dart behind a tree and freeze. She clutched the headphones tightly to her chest as she walked behind him, never taking her eyes off of him.

A surge of adrenalin flowed through her. It was exciting, she thought. The headphones were helping her prevent a murder. She would be a hero. She just needed some evidence.

The man finally turned off the main road and began walking toward a rundown old house that looked like it had seen better days.

"Creepy," Anna said to herself. "Who knows what he's keeping in there?"

When the man reached his home, he walked over to the side of the house and began picking up tree branches he had in a pile and carrying them into the woods. Anna watched impatiently for a few minutes, waiting for him to do something illegal or even vaguely spooky. Finally, he walked over to a truck that was parked in the yard and propped up on a jack. He grabbed a wrench from his toolbox and crawled under the truck.

While he was distracted, Anna figured this would be a good time to take a look in one of the windows of the house. She slowly stalked along the perimeter of the yard and crept around to the back of the house. She walked up to a window and peered inside, but was disappointed in the appallingly average-looking room. There was a coffee table with a newspaper on it, an old sofa, a faded armchair in the corner, and a pair of what looked like deer antlers hanging up on the wall above the TV.

A gruff voice from behind her startled her.

"Who are you?"

Anna whipped around and sputtered, trying to come up with something, so she said the first thing that came to mind.

"I, uh, need to use your phone. My cell battery died. May I, please?"

The man simply shrugged.

"Yeah, sure, go on in. It's in the kitchen," he turned back around and headed to his truck without another word.

Anna walked around to the front door and slowly pushed it

open. The rest of the house was just as average looking as the living room. She poked around the house, glancing out the window every so often to make sure the man was still at his truck. He was each time. He was clearly just fixing it. Anna sighed.

Then she noticed a battered door in the kitchen that presumably led to the basement. She marched over and ripped it open, flipping on the light switch. Hearing no noises coming from down there, she took a deep breath and slowly crept down the stairs. When she reached the bottom she looked around, anxious of what she might see.

But instead she instantly sighed and rolled her eyes when she looked around and saw nothing but old boxes full of junk and a warped ping pong table.

"Forget it," she said, stomping angrily back up the stairs. She walked out of the house and into the yard.

Noticing her reappearance, the man stood up and wiped his hands on his jeans.

"All set?"

"All set," Anna said. "Thanks, man."

"No problem," he said with a smile before squatting back down to the ground and continuing to work on his car.

Anna slowly walked back toward home, afraid to put the headphones on again.

*****

When she had arrived at the park once again, Anna took another look around. There was a couple walking their dog, two women laughing and chatting while their babies rolled around on a blanket on the ground next to them, and a few people milling about that she recognized from seeing them each day at the park. She also saw something else she recognized sitting on one of the benches: Mrs. Dunston's crocheted pink shawl.

Panic shot through Anna. What happened to Mrs. Dunston? Was that poor old woman next? Was this Anna's chance to prevent a murder? Anna grabbed the shawl and ran toward Mrs. Dunston's house as fast as her legs could carry her. At the very least, the old woman simply forgot the shawl on the bench and would appreciate its return. But there was now the possibility that Anna could actually keep her alive.

As she approached Mrs. Dunston's house, she was unnerved to see all the lights off. That woman's lights were never off. She went up the front steps and knocked on the door.

"Mrs. Dunston? Are you there?" she yelled out.

There was no response. Anna wondered if the old woman had been taken somewhere else. How would she find her? She felt sick to her stomach knowing that someone could harm a sweet old woman and leave her body somewhere no one could find. She ran around to the back of the house, frantically banging on windows as she went.

"Mrs. Dunston!" she screamed. "If you can hear me, make a sound! I'm here!"

Anna leaped onto the back porch and pulled at the back door. It was surprisingly unlocked, which sent her flying backwards. She quickly got up and ran inside, but the lack of any noise or human presence made her begin to lose hope.

With a quiet whimper, she let her shoulders droop. She looked at the headphones in her hand and slowly shook her head, feeling defeated. Finally, she solemnly lifted the headphones up and placed them on her head one last time, expecting to hear the old woman's final pained scream.

As expected, she did hear a scream. However, this scream wasn't Mrs. Dunston's. In fact, the scream was very particular. It was familiar. Anna dropped the headphones to the ground and fell to her knees, a choked sob escaping her throat.

This time, the scream in the headphones was her own.

Anna heard a noise behind her. She quickly stood up and spun around just in time to see Mrs. Dunston standing before her with a grim expression, raising an axe above her head. Anna screamed.

FRAN MAGLIONE

PARALYSIS

The dark shadow moved again - its existence only confirmed by the grumbling sound emanating from its chest. Sometimes it speaks to her, but that night it hadn't said a word yet. It just stood there, staring and growling.

Why won't you speak to me this time? She tried to talk but her voice died in her throat. Her lips wouldn't work, though she felt a ghost of movement there. Her breathing was labored as she struggled to stay calm. No sound came from her other than harsh breathing.

The shadow seemed to hear her anyway, and slowly made its way to her side. The creature reached out a blackened, boney hand and pressed hard on her chest, making her gasp for air.

She tried to move her arms and legs but they were firmly welded in place. There was a bit of feeling in her toes, though, so she hoped that if she wiggled them she could start to move the rest of her body. She struggled and pushed but nothing happened. To her right, her husband slept soundly, unaware of her struggle. He was sleeping on his side facing away from her, and the blankets slowly rose and fell with his steady breaths.

She attempted to will him awake, thinking as hard as she could, hoping that somehow her thoughts would penetrate his brain and he'd jerk out of his sound sleep and save her from this recurring hell. But there was no movement next to her on the bed. As usual, she was on her own. And when he wakes up later he will wonder why she's so upset and will never understand exactly what she endures night after night.

"It's just a dream," he always tells her.

"Dreams happen when you're asleep," she will counter. "I'm awake when this happens."

He doesn't get it, and probably never will. That's why she's on her own each time, and at the mercy of the shadow creatures.

Around her, the shadows swirl and inflate, taking on new forms that she can never quite see. Shapes appear but she can't recognize any forms, and they hide in her peripheral vision where she can't focus clearly.

"Don't touch her," one of the shadows said.

Another shadow swirled around and muttered a response she could barely hear.

"Just listen."

Listen to what? She thought to herself. Knowing she can't speak in this state, she simply gave up trying. They seem to be able to hear her thoughts pretty well anyway.

"The bells," another shadow hissed as it floated around the room.

She heard a slow thumping noise coming from the staircase in the hallway, as if something were making its way upstairs. It never ceases to amaze her how many of these creatures appear in her home each night, and how different they all are. She has stopped wondering where they come from. Instead, she thinks of more questions to ask them.

What bells? Where are they? What do they mean?

Laughter erupted from the shadow creatures.

"She never listens," one whispered.

The beast that was marching up the stairs finally stepped onto the landing and walked through the bedroom door. She couldn't see it but somehow she knew exactly what it looked like: matted fur, tall beastly legs, claws, black wings stretching far from each side of the creature. It's terrifying in its mere stature alone, but its dark eyes and menacing grin full of fangs just add to the terror. It represents every horrifying creature she's ever imagined. It's her walking nightmare.

It spoke in such a scratchy and deep voice that she couldn't make out a word. It sounded like the hissing of a snake with jagged rocks scratching across sheets of metal, with a deep reverberating rumble in the background.

I can't understand you, she thought.

"She never listens," another shadow whispered.

She tried to wiggle her fingers but nothing happened. Nothing ever happens, she knows this, but it doesn't stop her from trying every single time. The room had a static electricity in the air that tingled her skin, but not enough to allow her to move. It's the same deal every time, but she never seems to catch on.

The creatures hear her thoughts and laugh wickedly.

"That's what we've been telling you all along," one of them said.

"She refuses to listen to the bells," said another. "Your time is coming soon. Just wait."

My time is not coming soon, she thought, becoming agitated. My time won't be coming for a long time. You don't know what you're talking about. You never know what you're talking about!

Suddenly something sharp ripped across her stomach and she cringed, still unable to move. She could feel the warm trickle of blood seeping out of the cut and down her sides. It leaked onto the bed, and although she couldn't see them, she knew the sheets were tinged with crimson and blood was pooling around her.

Squeaking and chirping noises interrupted the silence as furry shadow creatures climbed onto the bed and crawled toward her. In her peripheral vision she could see them inching their way closer until they reached her legs. Tiny claws scratched and pulled her skin open as the hairy figures wormed their way into her body, biting and clawing her insides.

The onslaught of small creatures wouldn't stop, and her entire body was covered in prickly sensations and crawling skin. She desperately wanted to swat them away, protect her body, and grab each of the creatures and squeeze them until their insides oozed between her fingers. All she could do was lie there as they overwhelmed her. The woman seethed in her rage and growled.

She thought toward the darkness: What right do you have?

They all laughed around her.

"What right do we have?" They chanted the question over and over until it lost all meaning.

She decided she was through with them - the game was over. They continued to laugh and chant.

"You'll never be through with us," one of them whispered.

A dark shadow appeared in the doorway and floated across the floor to her side of the bed.

"Listen to the bells," it muttered.

She wanted to scream out loud, "What does that mean?" But, of course, she couldn't. The creature still heard her, though, and chuckled low in its throat.

"Just listen."

The creature took on the form of an old man with wrinkly skin. She tried to see him clearly, but all she could make out was thick layers of flabby skin. He leaned forward, hovering over her body, and his skin sagged. A small shadow creature jumped onto his back, and with a clawed arm grabbed a handful of skin from the back of his neck and pulled. The skin crackled and popped as it tightened against his skeleton. The woman felt her stomach turn.

The man grunted and wheezed as he tried to breathe. Pieces of skin flaked off his face and trickled down onto the bed. One piece slowly descended like a snowflake and landed in the middle of her face. She tried to blow it away in disgust, but her lips still didn't work.

A watery cackle came from the man's mouth as his lips peeled and split. Blood mixed with drool trickled down his chin. He stepped closer to the bed as the small creature still rode on his back, holding his skin tight in its fist.

The man raised a skinny arm with pulsating veins bulging through the tight, cracking skin above her head, made a fist and slammed it down onto her face.

The woman's body finally woke with a jolt in her bed. After a moment she could breathe again, and she wiggled her toes and moved her arms just to know she could. To her right, her husband groaned and rolled over toward her.

"Were you doing that sleep paralyzed thing again?"

She was still breathing heavily as she whispered to him.

"I think so."

In the corner, there was a hint of dark shadows beginning to move again, and the soft clanging of bells rang in the distance. The woman looked down at her stomach and saw her t-shirt drenched in blood, and the sheets around her were stained a deep red.

Her husband started chuckling and shaking his head.

"You never listen."

FRAN MAGLIONE

JONAH'S PEAK

The air took on a heavier weight as Brian and Lucy hiked deeper into the woods. The water in their thermoses sloshed around inside their backpacks with each step they took. What was a sunny, early winter day seemed to change the deeper they walked. Dark clouds rolled in overhead and the once non-existent breeze now sent the leaves flying through the air in mini twisters.

Lucy zipped up her fleece all the way to her neck.

"Think it's going to snow?"

"It wasn't supposed to," Brian answered. "I'm not sure where all of this is coming from."

He stopped and took out his cell phone to look at the weather radar. There was no service.

"Figures. These things never work when you need them. Well, I think we should just keep going. It's just a few clouds."

Lucy agreed, and they continued on their hike to the summit: Jonah's Peak. It was another in a series of hiking trails in the state that Brian was checking off his list.

They had only gone another few feet before a dozen crows flew by over their heads and landed in a tree just in front of them, cawing and cackling at them. Another strong gust of wind blew in and the sky darkened to nearly dusk. The two hikers paused briefly to brace themselves from the cold wind, and then continued on.

They hiked in silence, moving forward toward the peak as if being pulled there by an invisible force. Lucy was the first to break the trance.

"I think we should turn back."

The crows cawed at her in response.

"No," Brian said. "Let's keep moving."

The two trudged on through the leaves. The wind howled as they approached the base of the final climb to the summit. It was around half a mile straight up, but neither hiker so much as paused before starting the climb. They were both going to get to the top.

Suddenly, one of the trees behind them cracked and splintered. They turned to look as the tree seemed to take on a new form. It ripped its roots from the ground, and on tall and unsteady legs began hobbling toward them with branches outstretched.

Without a word the two ran, hopping over rocks and weaving and darting between trees. Their legs burned with the effort of running uphill but the tree creature was closing in fast. Its long legs brought it much closer with each step, no matter how quickly the two ran. Lucy looked behind her and stumbled over a fallen branch. Brian grabbed her and pulled her along.

"Keep moving!" he yelled.

Lucy saw an alternate path off to the side that was mostly overgrown and pulled Brian toward it and off of the marked trail. The two kept running, tripping over roots and rocks and holding each other for balance. They ran for what felt like miles before they finally stopped to breathe. Lucy bent over and gasped for air, resting her hands on her knees. Brian looked behind them and listened to the wind. Nothing was following them.

"I think we lost it," he said. "Whatever it was."

Lucy nodded and stood up, staring at the path behind them. All of it was unrecognizable, and what was left of the original path was nowhere to be seen.

"We're lost," she said plainly.

Brian sighed and nodded.

"Looks like it."

The sound of rushing water made Lucy turn her head. She started walking in the direction of the sound with Brian close behind. It didn't seem to matter that they were lost anymore. They walked for another hundred feet or so until they reached a clearing. The forest opened up to a babbling brook with a waterfall tumbling down rocks and feeding into it. Brian huffed.

"This isn't supposed to be here."

Lucy stepped forward and peered into the brook. Her reflection stared back at her, wobbling around with the current. Another shape in the water took her attention. She bent over to get a closer look when a bony arm jutted out of the water and grabbed her fleece. Lucy screamed as she tried to keep her balance. She felt Brian's arms wrap around her and pull her back, while one of his feet kicked at the arm, knocking it to pieces.

The two collapsed backward onto the grass while Lucy gasped for breath.

"What's going on?"

She didn't expect to get an answer to her question; Brian was just as confused as she was. She stood back up and offered a hand to Brian, pulling him to his feet. The two continued on without a word toward the waterfall.

It was wide and powerful, stretching across the side of the mountain ledge. Behind the waterfall they both spotted a pair of large, fluttering wings. Anticipating another attack, the two immediately ran without hesitation. The winged creature burst through the water and appeared on the other side, its feathered wings flapping loudly and flinging water all around.

The creature stretched its bony, furry limbs as sharp talons grew out of its hands and feet. It let out a pterodactyl-like shriek from its pointed beak and soared toward the two hikers. Brian and Lucy had a decent head start, but the creature quickly closed the distance with just a few flaps of its wings. Lucy ran slightly behind Brian, and the creature soared lower, reaching its feet toward her like a hawk attempting to capture its prey. Brian glanced behind him and saw the sharp talons getting closer. He turned and tackled Lucy to the ground just as the creature had closed in.

It squealed in anger and flew away, leaving the two hikers in yet another gasping heap on the forest floor. Their breathing was suddenly the only sound in the forest. They each took deep breaths, feeling the thudding of their own hearts in their chests. Gradually the thudding slowed down.

"When is this going to stop?" Lucy asked. "Every time we escape, another one appears. I want it all to stop. It's too hard. I just wanted to make it to the peak."

"I don't think it will stop," Brian said. "We're in too far. And I don't think we're going to make it to that peak."

Lucy's breathing began to slow. The sun had gone down and the air was beginning to freeze. She felt drowsy and her head began to bob forward. Content with not moving anymore, she gave up and let her body fully collapse against Brian, who was already beginning to doze behind her.

Lucy licked her dry, cracked lips and tried to speak, but her voice was raspy and quiet.

"I'm cold."

"Me, too," Brian said.

"How do we get out?" Lucy whispered.

Brian took a final gasp and exhaled deeply, whispering his final words.

"We don't."

*****

The search dogs barked and pulled in all directions as the police officers tried to figure out what they were leading them to. They came to a clearing near the base of the summit where crows cawed at them from the trees. An officer followed one of the dogs as it frantically began running onto an overgrown path off to the side.

"We got something here!" he called back to the rest of the squad.

They all ran over and found the two frozen bodies lying at the base of a tree.

"Hypothermia, I suppose," one of the officers said. "It got down to 5 degrees up here last night."

"That's a shame," another said, rubbing his forehead. "A damn shame."

"What made them think they could do this hike in this kind of weather?" the first officer asked. "Some folks think they can do anything, and then the world proves them otherwise - eats them right up."

"You got that right," another officer muttered. "Gotta stick to what you know. Now they'll never see that summit. Damn fine view up there, too, I hear."

The other officers nodded in agreement as they moved around the scene, careful not to disturb the two dead hikers frozen in each other's arms, eyes still open and full of hope for a beautiful view at the summit.

FRAN MAGLIONE

STORY TIME

"Stop it, Amy!"

Victor's whine resonated through the hallways of the top floor of the house. Amy rolled her eyes in annoyance.

"You're such a baby," she said. "What kind of 12-year-old gets that scared of a stupid story?"

Victor pouted and turned away, stomping his feet as he headed back to the stairs.

"You don't see what I do," he said over his shoulder as the giant, foot-long mosquitoes buzzed around his head. He tried to ignore the shadowy figure that was standing in the corner and staring.

Amy sighed and shook her head before turning back into her bedroom. She plopped down on her bed with a notebook and pen and continued writing her story. After just a few moments, Victor appeared in her doorway again.

"I need to know how it ends."

"It's not done yet," Amy said. "Probably won't be for a while."

"It's okay," he said. "Just keep telling it, please."

Victor sat down on the floor cross-legged and looked expectedly at his sister. A beast with long fangs and spikes sticking out of its back poked its head out of the closet, breathing heavily through its nose as Victor tried to ignore it and focus intently on his sister.

"Thunder cracked all around as the man sped through the neighborhood streets," she began. "Between flashes of lightning he could just make out the street signs - all streets he didn't even recognize. He immediately knew he was lost. He pulled his car over to the side of the road while he clicked open the map on his phone. Suddenly, he saw movement in the trees next to his car."

Victor inhaled deeply and pulled his knees up to his chin, wrapping his arms around his legs. He hated his sister's scary stories, but he also needed them. He needed to know how they ended, and if the creatures within them could ever be destroyed.

There were a lot of monsters following Victor around that he was just aching to get rid of. Some of them vanished eventually over time, but others seemed to follow him for years.

"The man rolled down his window to get a better look through the downpour of rain," Amy continued. "He called out into the night, 'Hello? Is anyone there?'"

Victor grinned.

"That's always a mistake. It's like walking down a dark hallway after hearing a noise."

"Right, but shh," Amy said. "The man paused and waited, listening for an answer. There was nothing but the rustle of leaves, until suddenly the wind picked up. Branches shuttered and leaves flew in all directions. Then, the man heard it: a loud thumping sound and a clacking of hooves."

Victor's blood ran cold, afraid of the creature that his sister would unveil. He risked a glance over at the creature that was currently in the closet and met his knowing look. There would be another added to the mix soon enough. He just hoped this one wouldn't mean the end.

He was sure there were ways to destroy the other creatures. There were endings to the stories. But this story didn't have an ending yet. Suddenly, Victor began to panic.

"Maybe I shouldn't hear this yet," he muttered. "You know, not until it's finished."

"Shut up, you already made me start," Amy said. "Maybe I can finish it as I go along if you would stop interrupting me."

"Yes, that's good," Victor said. "Try to finish it now."

In the hallway behind him, Victor heard a thump and a clacking sound of hooves. He tried to ignore it as Amy continued.

"Then, out of the bushes and tall grass appeared a hellish beast. Its front half looked like a deranged donkey, with large, thick teeth protruding from an underbite. It salivated, wheezed and grunted as it moved. Its back half was striped, kind of like a zebra but more mangy, and it's large horse-like hooves clacked on the pavement as it approached the street. Both halves of the creature seemed to move independently of each other, as though two separate animals were simply stitched together and were now trying to function as one. The back legs were long and stringy, and the front legs were short and stumpy."

Victor shuddered at the image and begged himself not to look at anything but his sister until the story was over.

"The creature ambled toward the man, slobbering and growling as it hopped. The man immediately rolled his window up and tried to start his car," she said.

"I'm sure it doesn't start," Victor said.

"No, of course it doesn't," Amy said with a smile. Outside the bedroom, the sounds of the creature crept closer.

Victor swallowed loudly and kept his eyes trained on his sister as she spoke.

"Drool dripped from the creature's mouth, and its long legs dragged along behind as the front legs stalked forward. Then, the creature hopped onto its hind legs and placed its donkey hooves on the car."

The loud squeal of something hard scraping against the metal of a car was sudden and deafening. Victor covered his ears and squeezed his eyes shut.

Amy reached out and grabbed his arms, pulling them free.

"How are you supposed to hear me, dork?"

Victor was hyperventilating.

"Hey, come on, little dude, it's not that scary," Amy said. She ran her hand along her little brother's back in a soothing matter.

No matter what Amy did, nothing seemed to calm Victor. His breathing grew quicker and shallower, his body trembled, and sweat beaded along his forehead and ran down his face. His heart thudded rapidly in his chest. Amy wrapped her arms around him tightly.

"Victor, you're scaring me. Come on, take some deep breaths for me."

"Finish," Victor gasped. "Finish the story."

"What? Why? You're terrified!"

"You need to finish it."

Amy stared confused at her little brother. Victor continued breathing heavily, trying to ignore the horrifying sounds all around him.

"Okay, um, well," Amy tried to remember where she left off.

"The car," Victor muttered.

"Right! The hooves scratched against the car. The man inside gave up trying to start the thing, and took off out the door and ran deeper into the woods."

Victor's breathing became even more labored so Amy continued quickly, speaking softly into his ear.

"Suddenly, the man saw a shotgun lying in the middle of the forest. He picked it up and fired at the creature, taking it down with one shot. The end."

"That's a terrible ending," Victor moaned. "That doesn't count."

"Sure it does, it's the ending. The story is over, the bad creature is dead."

The noises never ceased, and Victor could almost smell the foul breath coming from the creature's mouth. He jumped up from Amy's arms and ran out of the room while Amy gawked at him.

"It didn't work!" he yelled.

Victor ran down the stairs. He glanced behind him and saw the creature tumble gracelessly down the stairs in a mess of limbs and drool. One of its legs got caught in the banister on its way down and Victor could hear the loud crunch of bones breaking.

The creature was not deterred, and simply pulled itself up and limped toward him, dragging the lame leg behind it, continuing to wheeze and groan. Victor took off out the back door and into the trees behind the house.

Monsters were all around him now. Giant winged creatures from a story two years ago hung from tree limbs, furry snarling beasts from Amy's story a month ago stepped out from behind the trees and growled at him. The donkey creature had finally caught up to him. The leg that dragged behind was so mangled and bloody it was barely still attached.

Victor was completely surrounded by horror. He finally dropped to his knees and dipped his head to the ground in defeat.

If only Amy knew how to properly finish stories.

FRAN MAGLIONE

THE STATUE

Cold, dead eyes sharpened to awareness as the sound of giggling echoed through the forest. They blinked once, twice, and then returned to their vacant stare as two girls approached the burial ground.

Mira peered at her little pocket mirror as she walked, gliding a tube of crimson lipstick over her lips. She ran her hands through her hair one more time, making sure it was properly tousled.

"Okay," she said, turning to face her friend, "I'm ready!"

"You look great," Lillian smiled as she fidgeted with her camera, her shiny black nails flickering in the sunlight and her rings lightly clacking together as she adjusted the lens.

Mira adjusted her black stockings then attempted to yank her corset tighter.

Lillian chuckled.

"Be careful. I don't want you to crack a rib."

Mira stuck her tongue out before turning toward a gravestone. Her full skirt bounced and danced as she walked, the petticoats getting caught in bushes and branches every so often. The idea of a Gothic Lolita photoshoot came to Mira after she had heard a rumor of a centuries-old cemetery located in the middle of the woods a few miles from her home. She couldn't wait to pose in front of the tombstones and post them to her blog as soon as she got home.

Lillian's blossoming photography career would get a much-needed boost from the photos, she was certain. And even if it didn't, the trip would still make for a fun adventure with her best friend.

The woods grew eerily silent with each step they took closer to the graves, and Lillian felt her nerves starting to wane.

"Are you sure we should be going in there?"

Mira paused and turned toward her friend, confused.

"What's wrong? You don't want to do the photoshoot anymore?"

Lillian shrugged and fidgeted with her camera, swaying back and forth in place as she looked around.

"Doesn't this place seem kind of...creepy?"

"Well, yes, that's the point," Mira answered. "That was the whole idea behind the photoshoot. It has to be creepy. Now come on, you're being weird."

Mira walked toward the overgrown graveyard, looking around in awe at the old tombstones around her. Lillian sighed and followed, trying to keep up.

As they walked deeper into the cemetery they noticed that some graves were marked with large statues. There were angels and Jesus-type figures staring down at them all over.

"Wow, these are beautiful," Mira whispered.

Lillian raised her camera and snapped a few photos.

"Yeah, I guess this is pretty cool."

Suddenly, she saw something move in her periphery. She glanced to her left but saw nothing but tombstones and statues. One of the statues was of a beautiful male angel. He was draped in a cloth, and his large white wings spread out behind him as he stared down at the graves with an adoring smile. Lillian gaped at the figure.

"This one is stunning."

Mira walked over to see what she was looking at and immediately gasped.

"Yes! That one is perfect," she clapped her hands and

bounced. "Let's take a few shots of me in front of him."

Mira stepped into place near the statue and smoothed down her dress as Lillian started to tinker with her camera's settings.

"Now, remember," Mira said, "I'm a pensive, wistful, sad girl alone among the dead, so make sure there are no pretty rays of sunshine or brightly colored flowers in any of the shots."

Lillian rolled her eyes.

"Got it, Robert Smith. Put one hand on your hip and rest the other at your side. Now stare over at that tree."

The camera clicked away as Mira adjusted her stance, switching arms and altering her gaze with each shot. The shutter clicking abruptly stopped as Lillian stared above Mira.

"Did you see that?"

Mira sighed.

"See what? You're supposed to be focused on your subject, aren't you?"

"That statue behind you. I feel like it moved."

Mira turned around and glared at the statue.

"You behave, Mr. Angel. You're scaring my friend while she's supposed to be taking brilliant photographs of me, so cut it out."

Mira whirled back around with a smile.

"Better?"

Lillian pursed her lips and continued taking photos.

The girls moved around the cemetery pausing for photos in front of different tombstones and statues. Mira twirled, pouted, and smirked - the statue watched everything. With each step the girls took farther into the cemetery, the statue crept closer. Neither noticed until the snapping of a twig grabbed their attention.

"Probably just a squirrel or something," said Mira.

Lillian said nothing. She simply stared toward the entrance of the cemetery.

"The statue's gone," she whispered.

Mira's playful attitude faltered as she stood next to Lillian and stared at the grave stone once watched over by an angel.

Her blood ran cold and she whimpered.

"There's nothing there anymore - just the base."

Leaves crinkled behind them and the two girls spun around with a scream. The statue was standing right behind them, unmoving and staring blankly into the distance. Lillian turned and ran.

"Wait!" Mira screamed. "Don't leave me here!"

The two girls sprinted through the cemetery, hopping around the tombstones. They could hear the statue following closely, jumping over obstacles and propelling off of the tombstones with ease. But every time they turned around it would be standing still with empty eyes, not moving.

Mira was the first to figure it out.

"It stops when we look at it. Stop running and turn around!"

The two of them stopped and turned, staring directly at the statue. It stood in the grass, angelic and completely still in its original pose. Its intent was no longer evident. Lillian sobbed.

"What the hell is going on? How do we get out of here with this thing coming after us?"

"Maybe we could try walking backwards," Mira suggested. She stared at the statue and took one step backwards, then two. The angel did nothing.

Mira reached out and took Lillian's hand, guiding her backwards with her.

"We'll go as far as we possibly can like this," she said. "We'll be okay, I promise."

Lillian released a shuddering breath and started walking backwards with Mira, their feet shuffling through the leaves and their gazes never leaving the angel. They crept along slowly, unaware of the several other angel statues that were now approaching them from behind.

Another twig snapped and the angels were upon them. The girls had no time to scream.

*****

A warm summer breeze wafted through the forest. The only sound was two sets of footsteps stepping over twigs and leaves as they approached the cemetery.

June gazed up at the two angel statues in wonder, taking in the sharp details of their young pixie faces and graceful, flowing dresses.

"Cassie, come take a look at these. They look like they were just carved yesterday - incredible."

Cassie walked over to join her friend. As she approached the statues, her foot knocked into something hard, stopping her in her tracks. She bent over to see what she walked into.

"Is that a camera?"

Suddenly, a twig snapped.

FRAN MAGLIONE

BLURRY

"Wake up, birthday girl!"

Through the tiny slit in her eyelids, Tammy saw the blurry outline of her mom leaning over her.

"You're 10 years old today! That's a big deal," she continued.

Suddenly energized, Tammy sat up in her bed and threw her arms in the air.

"I'm 10!"

"Put your glasses on and come downstairs for your birthday breakfast." Her mom stood up from the bed and walked out of the room.

Everything was always blurry until Tammy put her glasses on. She hated them so much (they made her look like a dork) but she couldn't see a thing without them. But it was her birthday, so nothing else mattered.

Tammy went to the kitchen and gaped at the impressive breakfast spread her mom had prepared: waffles, eggs, bacon, toast, fruit. She couldn't believe it.

"Is someone else coming to eat?"

Tammy's mom laughed.

"Your 10th birthday is a big deal, sweetie. It calls for a special treat!"

Tammy's dad walked into the kitchen.

"Wow, is this the big birthday breakfast? Can I have some?"

"Sure! Everybody can have some!" Tammy proclaimed. She loved being the center of attention. She couldn't wait to get to school. There would be a cupcake party for her entire class, and she knew everyone would sing "Happy Birthday" to her and be extra nice to her all day.

The small family sat down at the table and dug in.

"We're so proud of our big girl," Tammy's dad said around bites of food. "Our little buddy is 10 years old! That's a huge deal."

"It's very special," her mom added.

Tammy put down her fork and frowned.

"Why is it so special? It feels like how every other day feels."

Her parents stopped chewing and exchanged glances.

"Well, it'll feel more special later, I'm sure," her mom winked.

Tammy still didn't understand, but she looked forward to whatever special things were sure to come later on.

*****

Water splashed over Tammy's face as she rinsed off the soap. She grabbed the hand towel and rubbed her face dry until she heard the sound of someone walking outside her bathroom. She glanced over, blurry-eyed without her glasses, but saw no one.

"Mom?"

No response.

Tammy shrugged and reached for her glasses when she was shocked by the sound of a man's voice she didn't recognize.

"Happy birthday, Tammy."

She jumped at the sink and looked over to see a tall, handsome man with dark hair and black clothing standing outside her bathroom. She could see him clearly: the wrinkles on his shirt, the flecks of gray in his hair, the slight beard stubble on his face. This seemed to frighten her even more than the fact that a stranger was in her home, because she hadn't put her glasses on yet.

Tammy stared in shock at the man.

"Who are you? And why are you so clear?"

The man chuckled but said nothing. Tammy grabbed her glasses and put them on, but the man had disappeared.

Tammy bounded out of the bathroom and ran screaming down the stairs to her parents.

"Mom! Dad! There's a man in the house!"

They both came running to meet her at the stairs, the shock evident on their faces.

"How can there be someone in the house?" her father asked. "We've been here all morning and no one's come in."

"I saw him, dad! He's upstairs! He was outside my bathroom."

Her parents exchanged glances again.

"Honey, you're going to be late for school," her mom started.

"Mom, I SAW him! He's up there!"

Her father sighed and walked up the stairs.

"Let me take a look."

He looked around the hallway and in the bathroom. He pulled back the shower curtain and opened the linen closet.

"No one here, buddy," he knelt down to her level and put a hand on her shoulder. "Time to get to school. You don't want to miss your class party do you?"

Tammy sighed in defeat. He had her there. She walked downstairs to her mother who was holding her backpack. Sulking, she pulled it on and went outside to wait for the school bus.

As the bus pulled away, Tammy's father sighed and turned to his wife.

"They don't waste any time do they?"

"It's her birthday, so technically they can start the process whenever they want," she turned and opened the door. "Come inside so we can pack her things."

*****

The day went just as perfectly as Tammy had hoped for. Her friends gave her handmade birthday cards, she got to choose one of the games during gym class, and everyone enjoyed the cupcakes at the end of the day. The grand finale was an epic rendition of "Happy Birthday," complete with a "How Old Are You Now?" refrain.

With blue icing staining her hands, Tammy ran to the restroom to wash up before dismissal. Her vigorous scrubbing splashed some soap onto her glasses, so she removed them to wipe them down with a paper towel.

"It's time, Tammy."

The young girl whipped around and stared at the man in black now standing behind her in sharp focus.

"This is the girl's room! You can't be in here!"

The man just laughed.

Tammy put her glasses on, only to see that the man had vanished again.

*****

The moment the bus dropped her off in front of her house, Tammy quickly marched forward and barged through the front door in a rage.

"Who is the man who keeps following me? And why can't I see him with my glasses?"

Her parents stood in the entrance, mouths agape, surrounded by Tammy's pink travel luggage. Tammy looked at the scene in anger.

"And what are you doing with all my stuff?"

Her father stepped forward, his hands raised in a placating stance.

"Wait, kiddo, what is this about a man you can't see with your glasses?"

"I can see him without my glasses on. He looks totally clear without them, but then I put them on and he disappears and I don't understand what's happening!"

Tammy stomped her feet and squealed, clearly on the verge of a tantrum.

Her father turned to face her mother.

"That doesn't sound right."

"They didn't say anything about that," Tammy's mother said. "In fact, they said they'd make their presence known to us before they took her."

Tammy quit stomping her feet and stared blankly.

"What do you mean TAKE me?!"

A sudden knock at the front door startled them all. Tammy's father pulled the door open and three men wearing dark red suits stood on the welcome mat.

"Hi there, we're here on behalf of the Dark Lord to pick up his daughter."

"Well, that's more like it," Tammy's father laughed. He reached his hand out to greet them all. "Thank you all for coming. Please, come on in."

Tammy's mother turned to the kitchen.

"Let me get you folks some coffee."

"We take it black," the lead man said. He turned his head and smiled down at Tammy who stared back at him in disbelief. He slowly walked toward her and knelt in front of her.

"This must be very confusing and scary for you, sweetie, so let me explain. These two fine people here are not your real parents. The truth is, your father is our Dark Lord, the evil incarnate, el diablo, if you will."

Confusion lined Tammy's face. Her fake father crept over to her.

"Honey, your daddy is Satan."

Tammy's jaw dropped. The strange man continued.

"You see, he wanted you to be raised as a human to keep your childhood innocence and purity. The deal was once you turned 10 he'd take you back and teach you his ways, leaving you a perfectly balanced creature who will one day rule the Kingdom of Hell and, expectedly, Earth as well. You'd have the advantage of having lived in both places. You'd have the best of both worlds, so to speak."

The woman who pretended to be Tammy's mother placed a hand on her shoulder.

"You see, honey? It all makes sense. You'll love your real dad, too, he's a swell guy."

Tammy slowly nodded, feeling oddly comforted by everything.

"But I still don't understand who that man was who kept showing up when I took off my glasses," she said.

The three men in red froze. The lead man spoke up.

"Was this man...wearing black?"

"Yeah, he was!"

He exchanged nervous glances with the other men.

"Oh, crap, Satan's not going to like this."

"How many times do we need to tell that stupid sprite that the child isn't his?" another man said, exasperated.

Suddenly the house began to rumble and shake. One of the men in red quickly pulled out a small wrapped box and handed it to Tammy.

"Here, sweetie, it's your birthday present from your dad. It's one of those fidget spinner things. Go outside and play with it for a while, okay? We need to...take care of something in here first."

Tammy smiled and skipped outside with her present. She plopped down in the grass and tore open the paper. Explosions rumbled in the house behind her as balls of fire flew every which way, and the sound of men shouting echoed through the neighborhood.

As she watched the bright pink object spin in her hands, Tammy wondered what other kinds of toys she'd find in Hell.

NOT WHAT IT SEEMS

The owl's head bobbed back and forth as Al maneuvered through the garden center at the home improvement store. It seemed like everyone he walked by had a fascination with the small plastic likeness in his hands.

A little boy squealed to his mother while pointing at the owl. An old woman giggled off to his left.

"Oh, that cute little thing won't actually work."

Al kept moving.

"You know what you gotta do with that?"

Al paused to face the burly, haggard man now standing before him, who resumed talking without waiting for an answer.

"You gotta move it around a bunch of times," he continued, "otherwise the animals will get wise to you. You make them think it's real if it moves to different spots throughout the day."

"Right," Al muttered. "Thanks."

Luckily, the young cashier seemed uninterested in the purchase as he dragged the owl over the scanner, its head still bobbing.

"Do you want a bag for this?"

Al pictured trying to navigate the parking lot and its

bumbling inhabitants while holding the owl and nodded quickly.

He grabbed the bagged owl and headed to his car, the owl's head still bobbing along the way inside the bag.

*****

"Did its eyes just blink?"

Al continued affixing the plastic owl to the back deck, groaning at Dave's question.

"Of course not, shut up."

"I swear to God, that thing's eyes just blinked."

Al rolled his eyes and adjusted the fake owl to his liking - twisting and turning it so it was facing different directions. He finally settled on having it face out toward the trees.

Dave chuckled.

"There's no way this thing could possibly work."

"You don't know that," Al said. "We've got chipmunks digging up our garden, birds making nests on our gutters, and I'm pretty sure that squirrel over there wants me dead. I had to do something, and since *someone* is so anti-poison…"

"You mean anti-killing innocent creatures, you beast," Dave growled.

Al poked at the fake owl's head, watching it bobble.

"I'll have to move it around the deck a couple times a day, otherwise the animals will start to catch on."

"Yeah, those chipmunks are pretty sharp."

Al continued ignoring Dave.

"Hopefully they don't figure it out. Keep an eye on it, and if we see a bird land on it or something we'll know it's not working."

Dave threw his hands up and walked back into the house. The owl nodded after him.

*****

Al finished his coffee and grabbed his laptop bag, heading

out to the deck before leaving for work. He had to move the owl first.

By the time Dave came downstairs Al was still standing outside, staring blankly ahead of him. Dave opened the back door.

"What are you doing? You're going to be late."

The words caught in Dave's throat when he saw what Al was staring at.

"Is that...an arm?"

Al crouched down and poked a stick at the piece of mangled and bloody flesh sitting in the grass.

"No way. That's part of an animal."

"Do we call the police or something?"

"I wouldn't." Al stood up. "Probably a piece of a deer. There's coyotes out here."

"It doesn't look like a deer..."

"Well, what else could it be? Are you telling me this is a human arm just lying in our backyard?"

Dave glanced at the appendage again.

"I'm not saying it's *not*."

"I don't have time for this, I have to get to work." Al headed to his car, yelling over his shoulder as he walked. "I'll toss it in the woods when I get back tonight, if an animal doesn't grab it first."

"Yeah, okay, sure." Dave turned to walk back into the house, pausing first to look back at the owl.

The owl bobbed its head.

*****

That night when Dave got home from work, the arm was gone and Al was lounging on the couch with a beer.

"Thanks for taking care of that gross thing," he said.

"That's what I'm here for."

Dave started getting dinner ready in the kitchen as the evening news played in the background. The typically perky female news anchor took on a melancholy tone as she spoke to the camera.

"Family and friends are continuing the search for Robert Francisco, the 39-year-old resident who has been missing for the past two days," she said.

Al yawned as he stood from the couch and turned the TV off.

"Is dinner almost ready?"

"It's getting there." Dave sprinkled some salt and pepper into the stir fry he was preparing. "Another 10 minutes or so."

"Okay, I'm going to go move the owl," he said as he headed out to the deck.

Dave watched him through the kitchen window. Al picked up the owl and slowly walked it to the other side of the deck. It almost seemed like he was whispering something to the owl. Dave chuckled and shook his head.

"Weirdo."

Al set down the owl and walked back inside. The owl bobbed its head.

*****

The next morning, Dave woke up first. It was still early - his alarm hadn't gone off yet and Al was still asleep - but something felt off. Dave quietly climbed out of bed and headed downstairs. He peaked out the back door but it was still dark outside. He opened the door and crept out onto the deck, stopping dead in his tracks when the foul odor of death attacked his senses.

"Oh, God."

Spread out on the grass behind the deck were what looked like two legs, and various discarded organs. Dave screamed then immediately vomited over the side of the deck.

Moments later Al came running downstairs and burst through the back door. He sucked in a breath.

"Holy shit."

"What the hell is this?" Dave raised his arms in frustration. "Why is our yard becoming a dumping ground for body parts?

What is going on?!"

Al put his arm around Dave and lead him back inside.

"Looks like it's time to call the police."

Dave pointedly stared at the owl as he headed back inside. It didn't move.

Al grabbed his cell phone and dialed while he rubbed his hand up and down Dave's back trying to soothe him. While Al spoke to the police, Dave tried to figure out how he would explain to the officers that he strongly believed a plastic owl was murdering people and leaving their body parts in the backyard.

Al hung up the phone and got a glass of water for Dave, encouraging him to drink.

"They're going to come over as soon as they can," he said. "They're pretty busy today."

"Busy? Too busy for dead bodies?!"

"There's been a few missing people reports apparently," Al explained. "And reports of wild animals roaming around town."

"Oh, great, so there's a wild animal out there killing and dismembering people?"

"Maybe, I don't know. Let's just stay out of the backyard until they get here." Al glanced at the time on his phone. "Look, you might as well just get ready for work. I'll stay home today and talk to them. You're in no state to talk."

Dave nodded and sighed.

"Okay, thanks. I'm going to go take a shower."

Dave climbed upstairs to the bathroom, turning on the water and pulling off his shirt. Before he stepped into the tub he glanced out the window. Flies swarmed the mass of body parts and the owl stood on the deck railing just above the carnage, his head bobbing in the wind.

*****

When Dave returned from work that night, the carnage was gone from the backyard and Al was inside on his regular spot on the couch.

"Did the police come?"

Al stood and walked over to him.

"Yes, they did. They collected all of the body parts as evidence. They said this kind of thing has been happening around the neighborhood. They think it's a rabid mountain lion or something. They have a bunch of hunters and search parties out in the woods looking for it."

"Were they really human body parts?"

"No, they weren't. They weren't even all from the same animal. One of the farms up the road is missing some pigs and goats, and their body parts can sometimes look human. Relax, it's just a crazy animal."

Dave was unconvinced.

"I know what human legs look like. Those were human parts back there."

Al sighed and put his hands on Dave's shoulders.

"Relax, okay? Don't let your imagination get the best of you. It's just animals. Animal control will find the cougar or whatever it is and they'll put it down. End of story. Now, all this talk of body parts is making me hungry. Let's start dinner."

Dave chuckled.

"You're such a dweeb."

Al pinched Dave's cheek.

"And you love it."

Al headed into the kitchen while Dave walked over to the back door and stared out at the deck. The owl stood on the railing as usual, unmoving with the lack of wind. Dave kept staring at the owl, waiting for it to move. When it didn't, he sighed and headed into the kitchen to help Al.

The owl slowly turned its head and stared at the back door where Dave had just stood.

*****

Dave tossed and turned most of the night, unable to get his mind off the sadistic owl on his deck. Finally he gave up and quietly crept down the stairs. He slowly opened the back door and tiptoed onto the deck. He walked up to the owl and picked it up, examining it briefly, turning it around in his hands and poking and prodding it. It was nothing but plastic, but it still creeped him out.

Dave carried it over to the tool shed and opened the door. It creaked loudly and Dave cringed and froze. Al was a light sleeper. Hearing nothing, he placed the owl inside the shed and slowly closed the door.

"Out of sight, out of mind," he muttered.

Quietly trying to avoid every creaking floorboard in the house, Dave made his way back into bed. Al hadn't stirred, and finally feeling at peace, Dave was able to drift back asleep.

Next to him, with his back facing Dave, Al laid awake. He waited until Dave's breathing evened out and quietly sat up and headed for the stairs.

Without hesitation, Al walked over to the tool shed and opened the door. He grabbed the owl and carried it back to the deck. After placing it back on the railing, he walked calmly back to the tool shed and grabbed a hatchet. When he turned around, Dave was standing in front of him.

"What the hell are you doing?" he asked.

Al stalked closer to Dave.

"Obeying."

"Obeying what?"

Al gestured to the owl.

"Oh, for crying out loud, Al, a plastic owl? That's your big master? Have a little dignity. At least get yourself a cool master."

"Like who?"

Dave pulled a large knife from behind his back and gestured to the lawn gnome nestled in their flower garden.

Al frowned.

"Wait, seriously? Have we both been killing people for our masters?"

Dave thought for a moment.

"I guess so."

The two burst into laughter. After a few moments, Dave calmed down and wiped a tear from his eye.

"I'll bet you didn't really call the cops that time either."

"Nope."

The two exploded into laughter again.

"This is so like us," Dave said.

"It so is."

The two finished laughing and dropped their weapons to the ground. With their arms around each other they strolled back to the house. They never made it through the back door, though.

*****

"So what do you think, Lieutenant?" the officer asked. "Are these our murder suspects?"

"Sure seems like it," he answered. "The neighbor said she heard two men screaming. Looks like someone got to them before we did, though."

Another officer walked over.

"Great, so we've got yet another murderer to look for now?"

"Probably just a vigilante that knew these two were the killers and wanted to get rid of them before they struck again," the Lieutenant shrugged. "Start collecting some evidence."

The officers milled around the yard marking off the bodies and taking photographs. On the deck, the owl sat proudly bobbing its head in the wind. In the grass below him, the gnome stood with a bright smile and a splash of blood on its face.

ONE FOR YOURSELF

"Just look at that sparkle, isn't that beautiful? Have you ever seen something so beautiful?"

"Never, Angela, that is stunning - just stunning. And even better, if you order this gorgeous bracelet in the next hour, we'll also throw in the rhinestone ladybug pin for just one dollar."

"One dollar? Are you serious? Now that is a deal, Liz."

"It sure is, Angela. These make perfect gifts for your friends or, heck, even for yourself!"

Both women exploded into a fit of giggles.

"We won't tell anyone that you spoiled yourself, and don't you deserve it?" Liz asked the camera. "Of course you do."

A bead of sweat began to form on Liz's forehead, threatening to slowly glide down her face and take a line of her makeup with it. Before it could fall, she flicked it away with her index finger.

"Now, Liz, take a look again at how this bracelet sparkles in the light." Angela twisted her arm back and forth under the hot studio lights. "It's hypnotic!"

"I just want to buy, buy, buy!" Liz choked out a laugh.

"And you do, too!" Angela yelled as she pointed at the camera. "You at home, don't let this deal get away from you.

Pick up that phone!"

"Pick it up NOW!" Liz added, her tone easing away from enthusiastic and veering toward desperate.

The impossible heat of the studio lights was becoming unbearable. The two women continued wiping sweat from their brows and trying to retain composure during the broadcast. A voice from backstage spoke through Angela's earpiece stating the name and location of a caller waiting on the line.

"Oh, it sounds like someone has called in! Beth from Kansas, are you there?"

"Yes, hello," an elderly female voice on the line answered.

"Hi, Beth!" Liz squealed. "Thanks for calling! Tell us just how stunningly beautiful you think this bracelet is."

"Simply stunning," the caller gasped. "I bought one for my best friend, Abbie, my daughter, Sarah, and my granddaughter, Megan."

Angela and Liz pumped their fists and cheered while nervously glancing off camera.

"Excellent! Thank you, Beth," exclaimed Angela. "This makes us very happy."

"It makes a lot of people here very happy," Liz added, glancing around her quickly. A tiny red light flickered off to the side of the set, making Liz squint and turn back to the camera. "Buying more would really help us. You like helping people, don't you?"

"Oh, yes, I sure do," Beth said.

"And, you like helping us...don't you?" Angela said.

"Uh, sure, I guess," Beth answered, hesitating a bit.

"Then buying more would really, REALLY help us," Angela continued. "So, what about you? You should pick one up for yourself to wear!"

The caller chuckled nervously on the line.

"Um, yes, I suppose that's not a bad idea..." Beth said.

"Great, we'll connect you with sales again," Angela said quickly, motioning to someone off-camera as the phone was cut off.

"We have another caller on the line from Connecticut," Liz said. "Barbara? You're on the air!"

"Hello, ladies," a cheerful woman said.

"Hello there!" Angela exclaimed. "Barbara, darling, how much do you love this bracelet?"

"So much!" Barbara answered. "It's so gorgeous! I just ordered it for my mother. It's her birthday in two weeks."

"Birthday, huh?" Liz asked. "Any other birthdays you know of coming up?"

"Oh, um, well," Barbara thought, "I think one of my cousins has a birthday next month."

"Perfect! Order one for her," Liz said.

"He's a man," Barbara said.

"Whatever, we'll connect you to sales," Angela snapped as she signaled off camera again and the line cut out.

"Okay, let's take another caller, shall we?" Liz said, eyes wide and voice getting shaky.

"Good idea," Angela said, holding her hand to her ear. "We have Margaret, from right here in Pittsburgh, on the line now. How about that - a local! Margaret? Are you there?"

"Yes, I'm here, hello," a woman's voice said.

"Thanks for calling!" Liz answered. "Now let us hear how beautiful you think this fabulous bracelet is."

"It's just breathtaking," Margaret said. "I just bought one for my sister in law - that's my husband's sister, Martha - and I just know she'll love it."

"That's great, Margaret, I'm so glad you bought one," Angela said, relieved.

"Why don't you go ahead and pick up another one for yourself?!" Liz shouted immediately. "Do you have any daughters? They'd love one, too!"

"Buy! Buy! Buy!" screamed Angela, giggling nervously.

"Oh, well, no daughters here," Margaret said, chuckling softly, "just two sons that are the spitting image of their father. One even took after his career for Pete's sake. Now I've got two police officers in the family. Can you imagine?"

The two women paused and stared at the camera, eyes wide.

"Police officers, you say?" Angela said calmly.

"Yes, that's right, my husband and son are both police officers. My son is a state trooper, actually."

Angela and Liz looked at each other. Off camera, voices murmured and whispered.

"Is your husband or son on duty right now?" Angela asked.

"Why, yes, my son is on duty," Margaret said.

Angela's jaw dropped while Liz emitted a squeaking sound and put her hands over her mouth, eyes wide again. Both women glanced off camera again, and then looked at each other.

"Well, isn't that wonderful!" Liz said with a smile. Murmurs and whispers could be heard off camera. The beads of sweat were ignored now, finally falling down Liz's face. "Does he ever watch this show? Does he know who we are?"

There was a pause on the phone while Margaret thought.

"Well, I do believe he's seen this program before," she said. "I'm always watching it when he comes over, so I wouldn't be surprised if he knew exactly who the two of you were."

"So, if we were to, say, show up someplace random and he happened to be there as well, completely by chance, would he...recognize us?" Liz continued.

"I don't...I don't get what you're trying to ask," Margaret sputtered.

The muttering and whispering off-camera increased in volume, becoming more agitated. Angela stared wide-eyed at Liz, pleading with her eyes, begging her to stop while nervously tapping on the table with her hand. The bracelet made a jingling noise with each tap.

"Could he pick us out of a crowd? If we were standing in a large crowd of people, scared and alone with all of our belongings --"

"Cut the mic!" a loud, gruff male voice snapped off-camera. Liz stood up looking around her in a panic. Angela stood up immediately after.

"Tell him to find us!" Angela yelled into the camera. "Tell all of them to find us! The highway, exit 3B! We need help!"

The two women bolted from the set as the camera feed cut off. A message appeared on the screen that read, "We're having technical difficulties and will be right back."

"Get them!" another man yelled out. "Don't let them leave."

An army of large men wearing navy blue blazers sprinted after the women, pulling out guns and trying to aim them at the moving targets.

Angela screamed and panted as she scurried behind Liz, panic beginning to overtake her. Seeing her distress, Liz grabbed Angela's hand and pulled her along toward the emergency exit and the two stumbled out the door. The building's alarm sounded and bullets whizzed by their heads as the men began to catch up to them. The women ran down the street until they reached a crowded block full of shops and restaurants. They saw a taxi approaching and Liz practically launched her body in front of it, frantically waving her arms and screaming.

The taxi squealed to a stop.

"Please help us," Liz said, panting and out of breath. "We need to get onto the highway, just to exit 3B. Please. We need help."

The taxi driver just shrugged and gestured for them to get in the car. The two women piled in the back and the car took off toward the highway. Liz looked out the windows and was relieved to see that no one was following them. She looked over at Angela with a sigh.

"We might have beat them here," she said.

Angela nodded, a glint of hope in her eyes.

"Let's hope that woman told the police," she said.

The taxi pulled onto the highway and sped along. After a few moments, the sign for exit 3B appeared in the distance. A string of police cars was parked along the exit ramp, lights flashing.

"They found us!" Liz exclaimed.

"Oh, thank God," Angela said. "They came through."

The taxi driver slowed down and stopped the car in front of the cops.

"This is just fine," Liz said with a smile, handing him a wad of cash. "Thanks for your help."

The driver nodded and took the money as the women climbed out of the car and walked toward the officers.

"You found us," Liz said, tears welling in her eyes. "Thank you so much."

"Everything will be okay now," one of the officers opened the door to his cruiser. "Just hop in and we'll take you someplace safe."

Angela and Liz looked at each other and laughed, hugging tightly while tears rolled freely down their faces.

"It's over," Angela whispered. "It's finally over."

"Get in the car, ladies," a gruff voice said.

The two women looked over and saw a man wearing a blue blazer walking toward them. He stopped just a few steps away from them.

"I said, get in," he muttered.

The women slowly let each other go, realization dawning on their faces. Liz started shaking her head as her body was wracked with sobs.

"No, that's not fair," she said. "It's just not fair. We were so close."

Several more men in blue blazers appeared and began muscling the two women into the back of the police cruiser. The first man walked up to the open door and pulled a rhinestone lady bug pin from his pocket.

"Don't forget one for yourself," he smiled and tossed the pin on Liz's lap, then slammed the door shut.

The cruiser pulled away from the exit ramp and headed back in the direction of the television studio.

ABOUT THE AUTHOR

Fran Maglione has been crafting creative short stories since the age of seven, which was also the year that she won her first national writing award. The accolades continued throughout her academic career and into her professional life as a local news reporter.

Though Fran has always had an interest in creepy stories and twist endings, she can neither confirm nor deny that this is a result of being born in Sleepy Hollow, NY. Frequent experiences with lucid dreaming and sleep paralysis probably have something to do with it, too.

She currently lives in southwestern Connecticut with her other half on a hill next to a river. Her hobbies include hiking, jogging, reading, taking photos, and predicting the ending of movies at around 20 minutes in. Her work has been published in *Dark Moon Digest*, as well as in her first book, *The Vixen's Scream: Stories for the Worst in All of Us*, both available on Amazon.

Author Site: amazon.com/author/franmaglione
Twitter: @FranMaglione
Instagram: @Fran.Maglione
Facebook: @FranMaglioneAuthor

www.ingramcontent.com/pod-product-compliance
Lightning Source LLC
Chambersburg PA
CBHW020640130626
46552CB00003B/1323